Tree-House Comix Proudly Presents

DOG MAN
FOR WHOM THE BALL ROLLS

WRITTEN AND ILLUSTRATED BY **DAV PILKEY**

AS GEORGE BEARD AND HAROLD HUTCHINS

WITH COLOR BY JOSE GARIBALDI

graphix

AN IMPRINT OF

■SCHOLASTIC·

FOR CHARISSE MELOTO,
WHO INSPIRES US ALL
TO DO GOOD!

Library of Congress Control Number 2019932354

978-1-338-23659-0 (POB)
978-1-338-29094-3 (Library)

10 9 8 7 6 5 4 3 2   19 20 21 22 23

Printed in China   62
First edition, September 2019

Edited by Ken Geist
Book design by Dav Pilkey and Phil Falco
Color by Jose Garibaldi
Color flatting by Aaron Polk
Publisher: David Saylor

CONTENTS

DOG MAN

Behind the Refined Sophistication!

Yo, SCOOBies!!! It's your old Pals George and Harold! 'SUP?

As you might have heard, we're supa mature now! And Deep!

The Thinker

We even got an AWARD for being so cultured!!! Check it out!

STUDENT AWARD

Our next award...

...is for MATURITY!

Thank you, Thank you!

OUR STORY Thus FAR

by Award-Winning Author George Beard

Illustrated by Award-Winning illustrator Harold Hutchins

Once there was a cop and a police dog...

KA-

...who got hurt in a big explosion!!!

BOOMERS

Wee-ooo-wee-ooo

They were rushed to the hospital...

...where the Doctor had Sad, Sad news!

Boo-Hoo

Sorry, Cop Dude! But your head is dying.

Weak!

Dog Man has three awesome friends:

ZUZU: world's greatest Poodle

Sarah Hatoff: world's greatest reporter

CHIEF: world's greatest chief

But there are complications...

Petey: world's most morally conflicted cat

One time, Petey tried to make an evil clone of himself...

Cloning Machine

Start

DNA

...But he got a good-hearted son instead.

Papa

Li'L Petey: world's greatest kitten

Petey tried to make his son become evil...

...but the Power of Good was stronger.

I'm afraid I can't be good. I've been so **BAD** in the past!

It's not about who we've been, Papa...

...It's about who we can become.

If Petey is going to be a good guy...

...he'd better hurry it up!!!

Because three **NEW** villains just arrived!

Piggy: Boss of "The FLEAS"

Bub: Flunky #1

Crunky: Flunky #2

Recently, they got shrunk to the size of Actual fleas...

ZAP

...and they could be hiding Anywhere!!!

scratch

scratch

scratch

scratch

Fortunately, Li'l Petey has been living with Dog Man while his Papa is in Cat Jail.

They share their home with a robot named 80-HD.

Together, the three friends have become a family.

A family who fights the forces of BADNESS!

What could possibly go wrong?

CHAPTER 1

Tree-
House
comix
Proudly
Presents

Rise OF THE PLANET OF THE CATS

Petey!!!

Petey!!!

cat Jail

Petey! Wake up!

You're on TV!!!

C'mon! You Gotta See it!!!

Last night's tragedy was narrowly averted...

...thanks to the SUPA BUDDIES!

But the biggest surprise of the night...

...was the heroic bravery...

...of Petey the Cat!

News

Fearless Feline

Check him out...

...as he saves this kid from the raging fire!

I'm so **PROUD** of you, Petey!!!

You're a **Hero!**

CUT it OUT, BiG JiM!!!

Heroes DON'T SNUGGLE!

Sorry, Petey.

News

Hero Dogs Pardoned

In related news, seven dog fugitives *Also* saved a guy!

The governor was so impressed, she **PARDONED** them!

Now all seven dogs are **FREE!**

Isn't that **Nice?**

Gee, that **IS** nice!!!

* French for: "Fight the Power, Baby!!!"

Meanwhile...

STOP, Thief!!

No way!

HUFF PUFF HUFF

WAIT UP!!!

HUFF PUFF HUFF PUFF

It's no use, Dog Man. I can't run anymore!

HUFF PUFF

STEP 1.

First, place your left hand inside the dotted lines marked "Left hand here." Hold the book open FLAT!

STEP 2:

Grasp the right-hand page with your Thumb and index finger (inside the dotted lines marked "Right Thumb Here").

STEP 3:

Now QUICKLY flip the right-hand page back and forth until the picture appears to be Animated.

(for extra fun, try adding your own sound-effects!)

O-RAMA

Remember,

while you are flipping,
be sure you can see
the image on page **29**
AND the image on page **31**.

If you flip quickly,
the two pictures will
start to look like
one **Animated** cartoon!

Don't forget to
add your own
sound-effects!

Left
hand here.

Who wazza bally wally?

Bazza wazza bally wall?

Who's a good doggy wazza bally wally?

29

Right Thumb here.

Who
Wazza
bally
wally?

Bazza
wazza
bally
wall?

Who's a
good
doggy
wazza
bally
wally?

Are ya **Ready?**

Let's RoLL!

Roll Roll Roll Roll Roll Roll Roll Roll Roll Ro

Meanwhile...

Oh boy, this is gonna be **Great!**

Dog Man's gonna catch the crook all by himself...

...now **everybody** will know what an <u>Awesome</u> cop he is!

WHAT iS WRONG WiTH YOU???

That's The THiRD Time This Week!

A BAD GuY ROLLS a BALL, You CHaSE iT, And he GeTS AWAY!

GO HOME, DOG MAN!

Tree-
HOUSE
comix
proudly
Presents

CHAPTER 2

BEHAVIORAL MODIFICATION THERAPY

Whisper
Whisper
Whisper

Okay, Dog Man. 80-HD and I are going to Teach you to **FOCUS!**

FLIP FLOP FLIP FLOP

We'll use These flash cards we made.

Every time you stay Focused, you get a <u>treat</u>!

But if you mess up, there's a <u>Penalty</u>!

You'll have to take a **bath!**

Splish splash

Flip FLOP Fli

Okay, now it's time to focus.

Focus... Focus...

focus...

Focus...

but then...

SPRONG

And so...

SCRUB
SCRUB
SCRUB

And Later...

SCRUB SCRUB SCRUB

...and after that...

SCRUB SCRUB SCRUB

...and so on...
...and so on...
...and so on...

FLIP-O-RAMA

Left hand here.

The good...

...the bad...

... and the Sudsy!!!

45

Right Thumb here.

The
good...

...the
bad...

... and
the
Sudsy!!!

Much, **MUCH** Later...

This is Taking a Lot Longer Than I thought it would.

SCRUB
SCRUB
SCRUB

But we can't give up, Dog Man!

We always gotta Keep trying!!!

And so...

SPLASH!

Dog Man

SCRUB
SCRUB
SCRUB

SPLASH!

Dog Man

SCRUB
SCRUB
SCRUB

SPLASH!

Dog Man

SCRUB
SCRUB
SCRUB

Tree-
House
comix
Proudly
Presents

CHAPTER 3

TO HECK WITH THE PLANET OF THE CATS

by the award-winning Award winners,
George Beard & Harold Hutchins

But, Piggy, ever since we joined **the FLEAS...**

...it's been one **DISASTER** after another!

And now we're so small, we can fit on a cat's whisker!

WHAT'S YOUR POINT?

Let's **QUIT!** I'm **HUNGRY!**

Me too!

We CAN'T QUIT **NOW!** I've got a **NEW** PLAN!

And So...

Petey's Secret Lab

Lab Sweet Lab

Kid-Sized Furniture

same day delivery

Luke and Andrew's Furniture

Petey's Secret Lab

MARKET

Fruit

Market

Art Supplies

Toys

Market

FLUFF FLUFF FLUFF

Dog man

GUESS WHO JUST GOT—

NO, DOG MAN!

Petey is my Papa, Remember?

Lick
Lick
Lick

GOOD boy, Dog Man!

Lick
Lick
Lick

You Learned to FOCUS!!!

GET OFFA ME NOW!

Hi, Papa!

Did you escape from jail again?

Nope! The governor gave me a **PARDON!**

Sweet!

And now that I'm a **FREE Cat...**

...You get to come and live with **ME!**

Isn't that **GREAT?**

Well? Isn't it???

But, Papa, what about Dog Man and 80-HD?

AW, don't worry about them! They have EAch other!

And now, **we** have each other, too!

oh.

So come on! **Let's GO!!!**

LET GO OF MY LEG!

Look, I appreciate your help while I was in Jail...

...But I'm free now. This is **MY KID**!

You **DO** want to live with me, don't you?

Yeah, I guess so.

Well, you don't seem too **HAPPY** about it!

Can Dog Man and 80-HD come and live with us?

No, they can't. It's just gonna be you and me from now on!

We're gonna build cool giant robots...

...and do all kinds of fun stuff together!

Can I still play with Dog Man and 80-HD and Sarah and Zuzu and...

Yeah, you can still play with those guys if you want.

Okay.

I'm happy!

69

Hey, Papa! Look at the cute flowers!

Those aren't flowers. Those are **WEEDS!**

Oh.

Hey, Papa! Look at the Pretty river!

That river isn't Pretty— **IT'S POLLUTED!**

Oh.

Hey, Papa! Look at all of the twinkly stars!!!

HEY! Watch where you're stepping!!!

There's **MUD EVERYWHERE!**

Oh.

Do you know what your problem is?

What, Papa?

You've been living with those two knuckleheads for so long...

...that you think the whole world is just **RAinbows** And **Unicorns** and **Lollypops!**

Yay! Lollypops!

But it's time you woke up and **FACED** the **TRUTh!**

You need a good dose of **REALiTY!!!**

CHAPTER 5

A good Dose of Reality

Soon...

PeTey's secret Lab

So this is the room where we'll build our robots...

...And our bedrooms are up here!

This is **MY** room...

Petey

...And this is **YOURS!**

kid

I'm not sleeping in there.

YOU'RE SLEEPING iN HERE AND THAT'S FINAL!

PLOP!

Lick

FLip
FLip
FLip

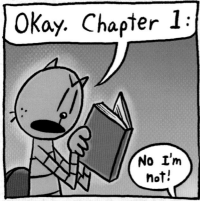

Okay. Chapter 1:

No I'm not!

ALRIGHT, FiNE!
iF YOU'RE GOING
TO ACT LiKE THAT...

...THEN NO BEDTiME
STORY FOR YOU!

Look, Kid— I'm trying to be good to you.

I wanna give you what **I NEVER HAD!**

When I was a kid, my Papa didn't care about me at all!

He took off and left my mom and me all alone!

He did?

Yep. And I never saw him again.

Hey, I know!

Let's find him!

Are you **CRAZY?** I Never wanna see that guy again!

But maybe he's sorry, Papa. Maybe he **Changed!**

Look, I know you think everybody is a good guy deep down inside...

WHAT'S THE BIG IDEA?

I thought I told you guys to let go!!!

Hi, fellas!

Petey's secret Lab

YOU GET BACK INTO BED RIGHT NOW!!!

Petey's secret Lab

Alright, listen up, you two...

...Maybe we can work something out.

Left hand here.

87

Right
Thumb
here.

CHAPTER 6

A Buncha Stuff That Happened Next

Meanwhile, back at Cat Jail...

...Big Jim was getting ready for bed.

Hey!

How come we have to carry you, Piggy?

Because I'm the **BRAINS** of this squad!

I can't waste my energy on menial tasks like **WALKING!**

Now **BUZZ OFF** while I work my **MAGIC!**

But how are you gonna do it, Piggy?

How are you gonna turn him into a cupcake?

I'M NOT GONNA TURN HiM INTO A CUPCAKE!!!

Hey, kitty Cat!

I've got a command for ya!!!

There's a speck of dirt in your left ear!

Get Rid of it!

99

Hey! Now that Piggy is gone...

Let's turn this cat into a **CUPCAKE!**

WAIT— I've got a **BETTER IDEA!!!**

Whisper whisper whisper

Petey's
secret
Lab

Pssst!

Sleepy Kitty

Shhhh!

Sleepy Ki

Thanks, 80-HD! I'm gonna go back to sleep!

When you find my Grampa, bring him back here, okay?

As a hopeful hero pierces the twilight...

...A Nefarious **NEW** villain Schemes in the Shadows.

RoBo-Time INdustries

Who is this New Newcomer???

And what **New** evil plans are up his newly pressed sleeves?

I'm NOT New!!!

It's Me, Dr. Scum! I was in the first book, Remember?

Oh yeah. Sorry.

Anyway, I've been designing an army of eviL Robots!!!

I call them CRiME CRABS!

They're Powerful enough to destroy the earth...

... but can they defeat Dog Man?

CHAPTER 7

Guess Who's Coming To Breakfast!

That morning before breakfast...

Petey and his son started building a new creation:

The Robo-Rat 2000.

Are you finished building that mecha-endoskeleton?

Almost. I just have to attach the cables.

Dad?

Well, don't just stand there like a **STATUE!** **INVITE ME IN!!!**

Hey, nice place ya Got here, Junior!

Thanks for finding my Grampa for me.

I owe you one!

You shouldn't put your dishes up so high!

It's **YOUR** fault they got broken!

Meanwhile...

Hello, I'm Sarah Hatoff with the News.

Today I'm gonna interview Chief!

Thanks, Sarah. It's a **GREAT** Day for the city...

... Because Dog Man has finally learned how to **FOCUS!**

Ya mean he doesn't go **BONKERS** when ya roll a ball anymore?

Nope! Allow me to demonstrate!

Meanwhile, at Cat Jail...

Hey, Bub!

What did you whisper into this cat's ear last night?

Well, my friend, There's an old saying:

"If you turn a cat into a cupcake, you'll eat for a day.

But if you turn a cat into a cupcake-themed superhero...

CHAPTER 8

The Old Man And the Sea-Food Crackers

Meanwhile...

Petey's
Secret
LaB

HeY! WHAT ARE you doing ?!!?

I'm making a book for my friend, Flippy!

FLIPPY 2
Electric
Boogaloo

128

PPPBBT!

WHAT ARE YA Tryin' to Do, Poison Me?

WHO TAUGHT YOU HOW TO COOK?

You shouldn't have done that, Grampa!

Why? WhAT do you care?

He's my Papa. I love him!

Yeah, well— Suit yourself!

I've never felt any love for that HotheAD!

Love isn't just Something you **feeL**, Grampa.

Love is Something you **DO**!

Sometimes you gotta **DO** it first...

...**THEN** you feel it!

WHO ASKED YOU?!!?

138

CHAPTER 9

BURGLE BALLS ATTACK

...And DOG Man can't stop me! **MWAH HA HA!**

DOG Man! There's a **NEW** villain in Town!

I'm Not New!

You must stop this **NEW** threat to Society!

come on! I was in the First Book!

Go catch the new bAd guy!!!

Seriously! I had a really big Role in Chapter 2!!!

And so...

COPS

Uh-oh!

We gotta go save the world, Papa!

Hey! That's a Good idea! You Guys should Go!

Make me proud, Son!

And So...

Petey's secret Lab

CHAPTER 10
DO GOOD

Maturity Award Winner
By George Beard and

Maturity Award Winner
Harold Hutchins

150

And So...

Here they come, Papa!

If we're gonna stop those guys...

...we all have to work together!

I'll be Right bAck!

PLUP

Knock Knock
Knock

You're a good boy, Dog Man...

...But that doesn't mean very much.

Look around.

This city is **Filled** with good people...

...but none of them are **DOING** Anything!

It's not enough to just **BE GOOD.**

Gee, I sure wish 80-HD was—

—here.

Okay, Papa! Get Ready!!!

Here Come The SUPA BUDDIES!

GRRRRRR!

RUFF RUFF RUFF

RUFF RUFF RUFF

FLiP, BABY, FLiP!

Left hand here.

Right
Thumb
here.

Tree-House Comix Proudly Presents

CHAPTER 11

The Very Hangry Raterpillar

Soon, the Very Hangry Raterpillar chased the last remaining Burgle Ball...

... Straight to Dr. Scum's Laboratory.

ROBO-TIME Industries

GULP!

RATS! All of my Burgle Balls got eaten up!!!

But No worries! That Raterpillar is No match for...

Right
Thumb
here.

CHAPTER 12

A Farewell to Arms

MWAH HA HA HA HA!!!

Petey and the very Hangry Raterpillar were now encased in a charcoal **TOMB**...

...and nearly everyone on the street below was <u>Horrified</u>!

Don't worry, nearly everyone...

I think I know what's going to happen!

whisper whisper whisper

Meanwhile...

MUSEUM

Special Exhibit
THE HOPE
MOOD RING

Rare 'n' Ancient   WARNING: May be cursed!!!

Okay, Daryl...

...here's the plan:

You're going to lower me down into that museum...

...and I'm going to steal the world-famous "Hope Mood Ring"!

But, Piggy—we can't steal! We're the **FRIENDLY FRIENDS!**

Did I say **STEAL?** I meant "PROTECT"!

Ya see, a bunch of Robbers are gonna try to steal it...

...and we have to foil their evil schemes!

AWESOME! FoiL is SHINY!!!

Riiight! Now Lower me into that vent...

...And don't Pull me up until you get my signal!

OK!

The Terrified cries for help echoed across the rooftops...

... and fell upon the ears of a hungry, hungry hero!

CHAPTER 13

COMMANDER CUPCAKE RETURNS

As the soft, pink dusk of twilight blankets the city...

...one vigilant soul heeds the sounds of despair...

HELP!
HELP!

...And bravely responds.

Masked in the deep shadows of the surrendering sun...

...and armed only with an unquenchable appetite...

...for cupcakes...

SAL'S CUPCAKE KITCHEN

...Our spunky spartan of sprinkles barges forth where even the most valiant fear to tiptoe!

Um—That's not really helping!

Meanwhile, off in the distance, encased in a silent Sepulchre of cinders...

... a startling transmogrification...

...crackles to life from its carbon Chrysalis.

CRACK!

POP

Aw, come on!!!

Hey, Look! That cupcake-themed superhero just captured the new villain!!!

How'd ya do it?

Well, I—

And Look! He just captured **PiGGY!**

And he's recovered the stolen **HOPE MOOD RiNG!!!**

Gee, it's too bad he didn't capture **ALL** of the **FLEAS!!!**

Yeah! I wonder whatever happened to Crunky and Bub?

Hmmm—

Here they are!

Did we miss anything???

Ya sure did! Commander Cupcake just solved the crimes of the century!!!

HOORAY FOR COMMANDER CUPCAKE!!!

Wait, what?

What's wrong, Papa?

It's NOT FAIR! We did all of the work...

...and that cupcake GUY got all the **CREDIT!**

It doesn't matter, Papa. Everything still worked out okay!

Oh yeah, I forgot! You're "Mr. Rainbows and Unicorns"!!!

And Lollypops!

ALRight, be my Guest! Keep your head up there in the stars!!!

The only Problem is, there's a Lotta **MUD** down there, PaL!

Hey, Look!

I have no idea!

Well, we're home!

HEY!!!

What happened?

Where?

You're gonna stay at Dog Man's house this weekend, Remember?

But, Papa—

NO! We made a promise and we're Gonna keep it!!!

And so...

You wanna know something, kid?

What, Papa?

This world has a lot of problems...

...But it could never be a horrible place...

I'll come back on Sunday niGht to pick you up, okay?

Hey, Papa- You should stay with us this weekend!

No way! I'm GoinG home! I've Got **BiG PLANS** for that place!

But you don't have a bed to sleep in. Or a Pillow. Or a blanket!

splish splash splish splash splish splash splish splash

Menu ☰

SARAH **HAT OFF** NEWS BLOG *WITH SARAH HATOFF*

COMMANDER CUPCAKE CAPTURES CROOKS BY CONSUMING CARBS!

Move over, Supa Buddies, there's a new superhero in town! Last night, Commander Cupcake amazed the world by single-handedly capturing not only the FLEAS, but an all-new villain named Dr. Scum. When asked to comment, Commander Cupcake said, "Ask not what cupcakes can do for you, ask what YOU can do for cupcakes. Amen." The mayor has declared today COMMANDER CUPCAKE DAY and is encouraging all citizens to help fight crime by eating as many cupcakes as possible.

CAT BURGLAR APPREHENDED

An elderly cat was caught selling stolen goods out of the back of his rental truck last night. He was charged with possession of stolen property, and totally missing the point of this book.

"Wait," said the elderly cat. "There was a point to this book?"

by George and Harold

☆ The title of this book (and the titles of Chapters 8 and 12) were inspired by the books of Ernest Hemingway.

☆ Panels #2 and #3 from page 50 are direct Quotes from <u>For Whom the Bell Tolls</u> by Ernest Hemingway (who was A <u>supa</u> cat Lover).

☆ The Very Hangry Raterpillar was inspired by one of our All-Time Favorite books: <u>The Very Hungry Caterpillar</u> by Eric Carle.

☆ Big Jim was named after a 1970s action figure.

☆ Harold, who usually only illustrates these books, helped write the story for this one.

☆ One of the themes of this book was inspired by Harold's favorite short poem:

Two men looked through prison bars.
One saw mud. The other, stars.

— author unknown (but variations are
often attributed to Dale Carnegie
and/or Reverend Frederick Langbridge)

HOW 2 DRAW

COMMANDER CUPCAKE

in **42** Ridiculously easy Steps!

HOW 2 DRAW

PAPA AND THE KID

in **39** Ridiculously easy steps!!!

229

Turn the page to give these two fellas a ride on the back of a **RATTERFLY!!!**

Erase
Petey's
back
Leg →

HOW 2 DRAW DOG MAN

in 26 Ridiculously easy steps!

GET READING W